BLACK SOX THE FOX
A Week at the Beach

written by
Jodi Beasley

Illustrated by
Mauro Lirussi

Illustrations by Mauro Lirussi

First printing 2021.

ISBN 978-1-7365084-0-4 (Print/Hardback)
ISBN 978-1-7365084-1-1 (Print/Paperback)
ISBN 978-1-7365084-2-8 (eBook)

Contact Author at:
booksbybeasley@gmail.com

BLACK SOX THE FOX
A Week at the Beach

written by
Jodi Beasley

Illustrated by
Mauro Lirussi

Written with fond memories of our family vacation to Murrell's Inlet, SC in 2020 and our adorable fox friend.

On a beautiful beach in the south lives an adorable, but curious, fox named Black Sox. Each week Black Sox busies himself with everyone else's business......

On Sunday, Black Sox anxiously awaits his new friends arrival while hiding in the tall beach grass. He watches them unload their stuffed cars with backpacks, pillows, and beach toys! He can hardly wait to meet them! But, wait......

On Monday, Black Sox watches his new friends play at the beach while hiding behind a large mountain shaped sand dune. The older children are flying rainbow colored kites and passing a yellow disc. Meanwhile, the younger children are hunting shells.

Black Sox SO badly wants to show them his huge and amazing shell collection. But, remember......

On Tuesday, Black Sox spies on his buddies sandcastle contest from under the boardwalk, wishing he could join in the fun! Black Sox is the best at digging the deepest motes! But, remember......

Black Sox ONLY comes out at night!

On Wednesday, Black Sox watches closely as the family strolls down the boulevard to the mini golf course. Black Sox hides behind the pirate ship watching his pals' putting competition. He would love to show off his superb hole in one skills! But, remember......

Black Sox ONLY comes out at night!

On Thursday, Black Sox hurries to the edge of the beach grass to observe his chums racing golf carts up and down the beach boulevard. My, how he wishes he could ride shotgun! He would be the coolest co-pilot! But, remember......

Black Sox ONLY comes out at night!

On Friday, Black Sox stares at his amigos and licks his chops at the smell of their dinner sizzling on the grill. Oh, how he would adore the taste of one of those juicy hot dogs! (hot dogs ARE his favorite) But, remember......

On Saturday, Black Sox excitedly gazes at his pals' glow in the dark pool party. He is so excited because it is getting darker by the minute. He has been working SO hard on his cannonball!!

Now, remember......

Black Sox ONLY comes out at night!

Black Sox ONLY comes out at night!

On Sunday, Black Sox is full of sadness as his friends are packing and loading their cars. Soon all is empty and quiet.

......Car doors slam and new friends unload! How thrilled he is to have new pals for the week! He can't wait to introduce himself!

But remember......

Black Sox ONLY comes out at night!